For Tom and Alice I.W.

For Alyx with love R.A.

Four Winds Press
Macmillan Publishing Company
866 Third Avenue
New York, NY 10022

First published 1991 in Great Britain by Walker Books, Ltd, London
First American edition 1991
Printed and bound in Hong Kong by South China Printing Company (1988) Ltd.
10 9 8 7 6 5 4 3 2 1

Library of Congress Cataloging-in-Publication Data is available.
ISBN 0-02-792741-5

Quacky quack-quack!

Written by Ian Whybrow

Illustrated by Russell Ayto

Four Winds Press
New York

This little baby had some bread;

His mommy gave it to him for the ducks,

but he started eating it instead.

Lots of little ducky birds
came swimming along,
thinking it was feeding time,
but they were wrong!

The baby held on to the bag,
he wouldn't let go;
And the crowd of noisy ducky birds
started to grow.
They made a lot of ducky noises…

quacky quack-quack!

Then three fat geese swam up
and went honk! honk! at the back.

And when a band went marching by,
in gold and red and black,
Nobody could hear the tune –
just . . .

"Louder, boys," said the bandmaster,
"give it a bit more puff."
So the band went **toot! toot!** ever so loud,
but it still wasn't loud enough.

Then all over the city, including the city zoo,
the animals heard the noise
and started making noises too.
All the donkeys went...

All the dogs went...

WOof! WOof!

All the snakes went...

SSS—SSSS!

All the crocodiles went…

snap! snap!

All the mice went…

squeaky ~ squeaky

All the lions went...

roar!

Then one little boy piped up and said,
"I know what this is about.
That's my baby brother with the
bag of bread;
I'll soon have this sorted out."

He ran over to where the baby
was holding his bag of bread
and not giving any to the birdies,
but eating it instead.

And he said, "What about some
for the ducky birds?"
But the baby started to...

scream!

So his brother said,
"Let me hold the bag,
and I'll let you hold my ice cream."

Then the boy said,
"Quiet, all you quack-quacks!
You're all going to get fed."
And he put his hand in the paper bag
and brought out a handful of bread.

So all the birds went quiet...

and the   band stopped playing too...

And all the animals stopped making a noise,
including the animals in the zoo.

And that's when the baby realized
they were all waiting for a crumb!
So he took a great big handful
of bread, and…

all the ducky birds some.

Then all the hungry birdies
were ever so glad they'd come,
And instead of going…

honk! honk!
quacky quack-
quack!

all the birdies said…

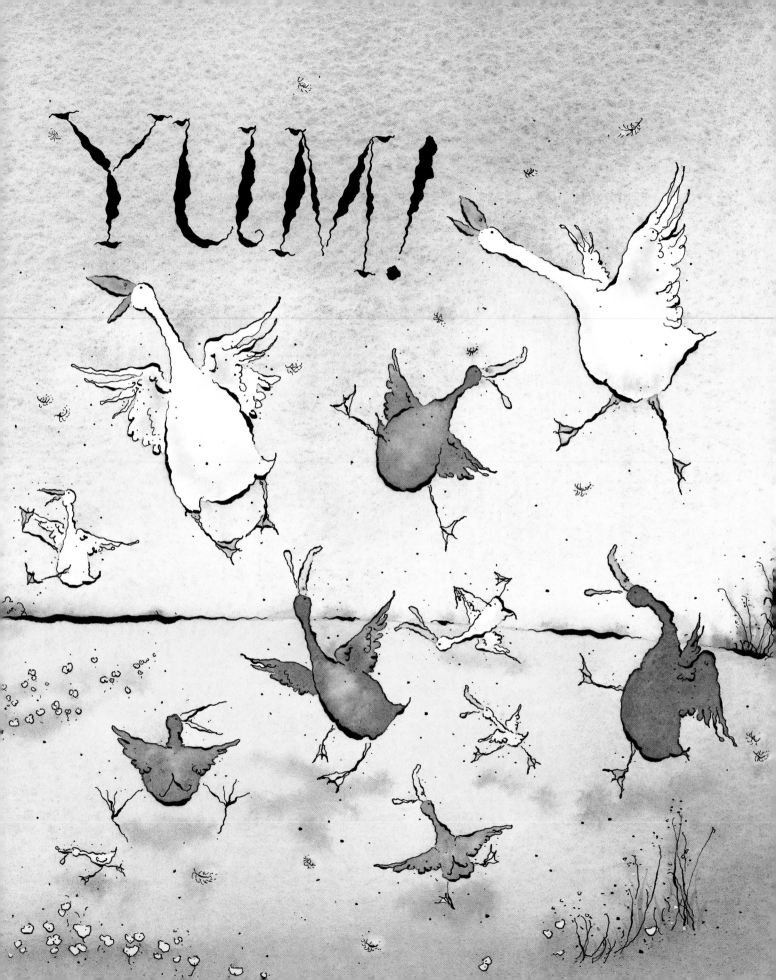